This book belongs to:

_____

First published in Great Britain in 1980 by Andersen Press Ltd.,
20 Vauxhall Bridge Road, London SW1V 2SA.
This paperback edition first published in 2015 by Andersen Press Ltd.
Copyright © David McKee, 1980.
The rights of David McKee to be identified as the author and illustrator of this work have been
asserted by him in accordance with the Copyright, Designs and Patents Act, 1988.
All rights reserved. Printed and bound in China.

7   9   10   8

British Library Cataloguing in Publication Data available.

ISBN 978 1 78344 290 4

NOT NOW, BERNARD

ANDERSEN PRESS

"Hello, Dad," said Bernard.

"Not now, Bernard," said his father.

"Hello, Mum," said Bernard.

"Not now, Bernard," said his mother.

"There's a monster in the garden and it's going to eat me," said Bernard.

"Not now, Bernard," said his mother.

Bernard went into the garden.

"Hello, monster," he said to the monster.

The monster ate Bernard up, every bit.

Then the monster went indoors.

"ROAR," went the monster behind
Bernard's mother.

"Not now, Bernard," said Bernard's mother.

The monster bit Bernard's father.

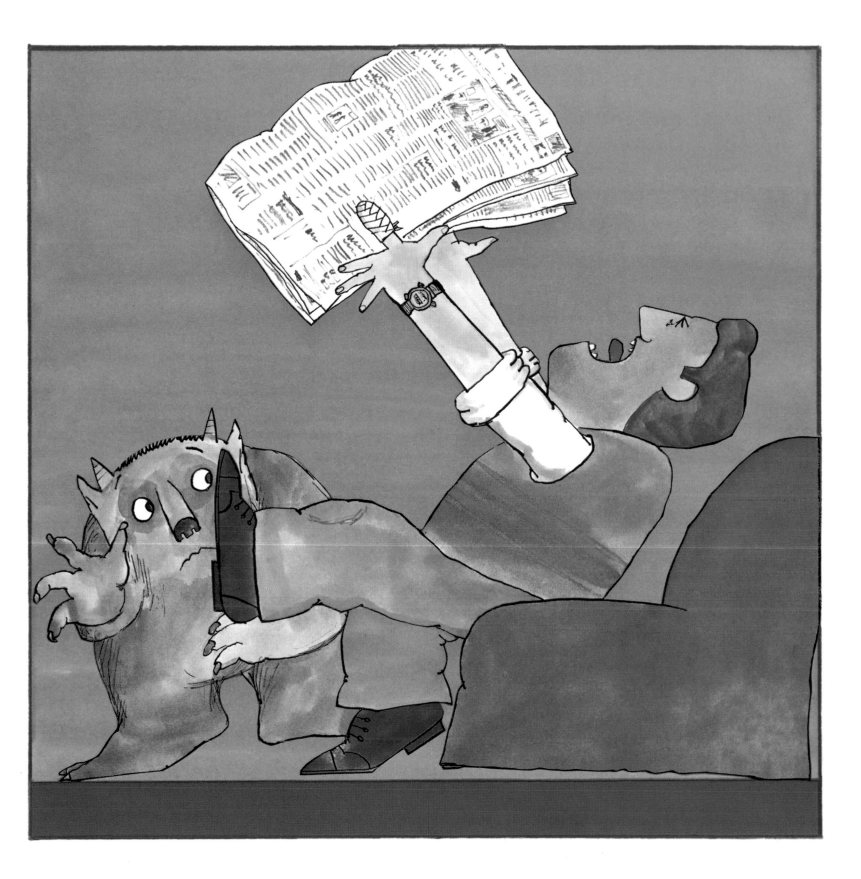

"Not now, Bernard," said Bernard's father.

"Your dinner's ready," said Bernard's mother.

She put the dinner in front of the television.

The monster ate the dinner.

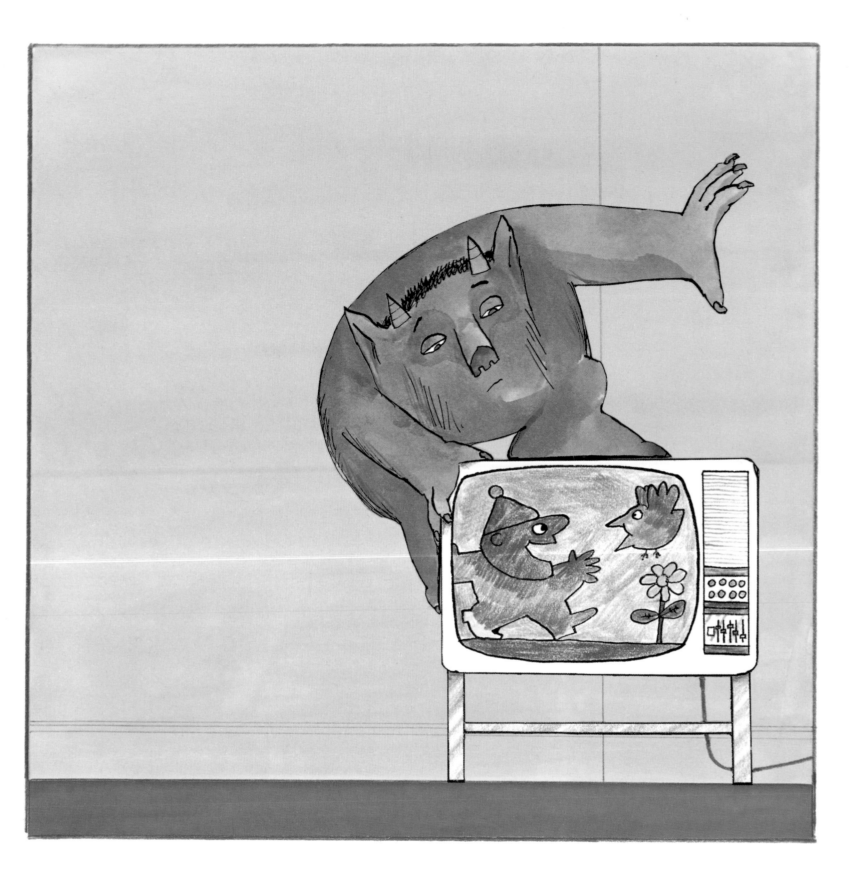

Then it watched the television.

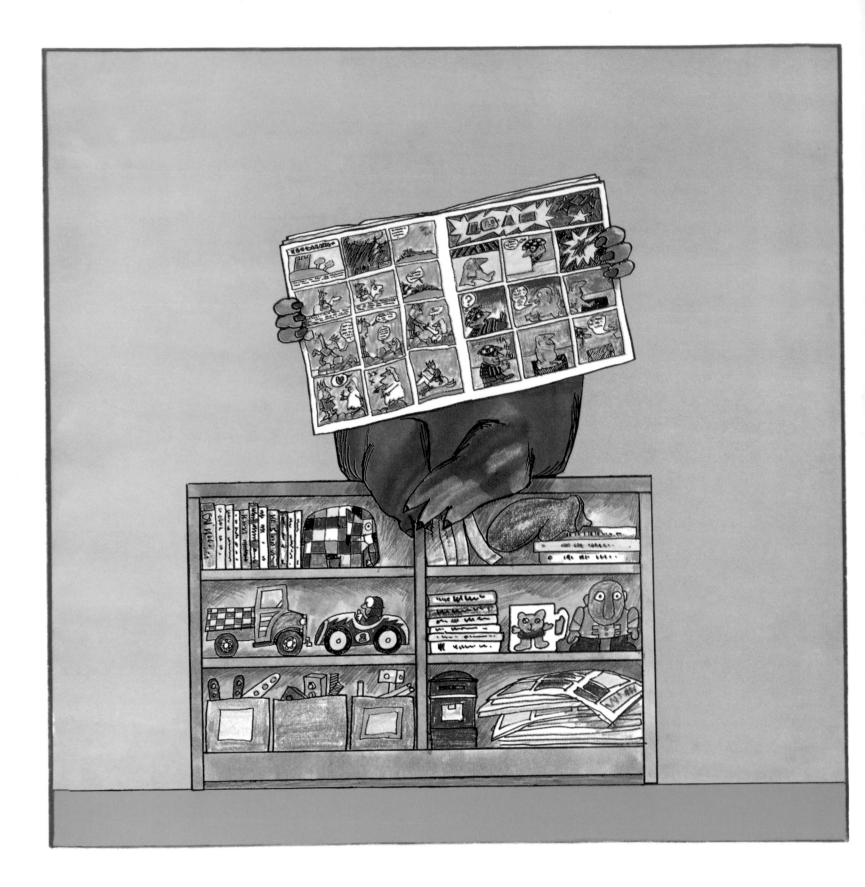

Then it read one of Bernard's comics.

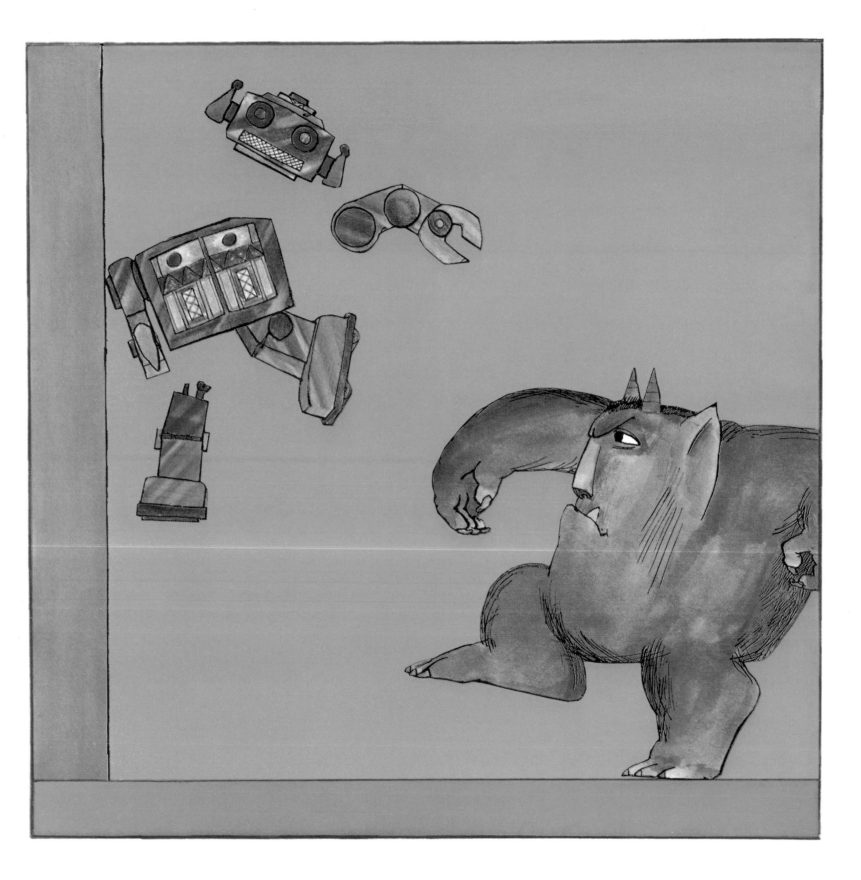

And broke one of his toys.

"Go to bed. I've taken up your milk," called
Bernard's mother.

The monster went upstairs.

"But I'm a monster," said the monster.

"Not now, Bernard," said Bernard's mother.

Discover more
DAVID MCKEE
classics...